Ladybird Readers

Snow White
and the
Seven Dwarfs

Text adapted by Sorrel Pitts
Illustrated by Tanya Maiboroda
Series Editor: Sorrel Pitts

LADYBIRD BOOKS

UK | USA | Canada | Ireland | Australia
India | New Zealand | South Africa

Ladybird Books is part of the Penguin Random House group of companies
whose addresses can be found at global.penguinrandomhouse.com.
www.penguin.co.uk   www.puffin.co.uk   www.ladybird.co.uk

Penguin
Random House
UK

First published 2018
001

Copyright © Ladybird Books Ltd, 2018

Printed in China

A CIP catalogue record for this book is available from the British Library

ISBN: 978-0-241-31955-0

All correspondence to
Ladybird Books
Penguin Random House Children's
80 Strand, London WC2R 0RL

MIX
Paper from
responsible sources
FSC® C018179
FSC
www.fsc.org

Ladybird Readers

Snow White
and the
Seven Dwarfs

Picture words

Snow White

king

queen

prince

huntsman

dwarf

magic mirror

forest

ribbons

comb

apples

angry

5

A beautiful queen had a baby girl.

The baby's skin was as white as snow, and she had beautiful black hair.

The queen called her baby Snow White.

Soon, the queen died, and
the king got married again.

The new queen had a magic
mirror. "Who is the most
beautiful woman in the world?"
she asked it.

The mirror said, "You are."

Soon, Snow White was a beautiful young woman.

One day, the queen spoke to her mirror. "Who is the most beautiful woman in the world?" she asked it.

The mirror said, "Snow White is the most beautiful woman in the world."

The queen was angry.
She didn't want to live
with a woman who was
more beautiful than her.

"Take Snow White into the
forest, and kill her," she said
to her huntsman.

The huntsman took Snow White into the forest, but he couldn't kill her.

"Run!" he said. "The queen wants to kill you. You must never go home."

Snow White ran and ran.
Soon, she came to a little house.
She went inside, because she
was very tired.

In the house, she saw seven
little chairs and seven
little beds.

Snow White went to sleep
on the beds.

Soon, the dwarfs who lived
in the house came home.

"Why is this beautiful woman
in our house?" they asked.

19

Snow White woke up. "Who are you?" she said.

"We are the seven dwarfs," said one dwarf. "We work in the forest."

"The bad queen wants to kill me," Snow White said.

The dwarfs thought for a
few seconds.

Then, one of the dwarfs said,
"You can stay here. Don't open
this door, or speak to people
who come to it."

That evening, the queen asked her mirror, "Who is the most beautiful woman in the world?"

"Snow White," it said.

The queen was angry. She put on different clothes, went into the forest, and found the little house.

"Come and see my
beautiful ribbons,"
said the queen.

Snow White looked
at the ribbons.

Then, the queen put one
ribbon round Snow White's
neck. The ribbon hurt!

The dwarfs came home and found Snow White on the floor. Was she dead?

No—she woke up!

"Snow White is the most beautiful woman in the world," the mirror said to the queen that evening.

The queen was very angry,
and she took some combs
to the house.

"Look at my beautiful
combs," she called.

"I mustn't speak to people
who come to the door,"
said Snow White.

"Then I can leave a comb here," said the queen.

The queen left. Snow White put the comb in her hair, and fell to the floor.

The dwarfs came home, and took the comb from Snow White's hair. Soon, she woke up.

"Who is the most beautiful woman in the world?" the queen asked the mirror again.

"Snow White," it said.

The queen was now very angry. "Tonight I must kill her!" she said, and she went to the little house again.

Snow White was in the house,
and the door was open.
She saw a woman with
some apples.

"Come and eat my
beautiful apples,"
said the woman.

Snow White went to the
woman, and took an apple.

When Snow White ate the apple,
she fell to the floor.

The dwarfs came back, and tried
to help Snow White, but they
could not wake her up.

The dwarfs were very sad.

The dwarfs put Snow White
into a glass box.

That day, a prince rode past.
He saw Snow White in the box.

"She is sleeping," he thought.
Then, he fell in love with her,
because she was very beautiful.

The prince kissed Snow White, and she opened her eyes.

"Please be my wife," he said.

Snow White fell in love with the prince. "Of course!" she said.

Very soon, Snow White and
the prince got married.

When the bad queen saw
Snow White, she was very
angry, and she ran into the forest.
People did not see her again.

Snow White and the prince, and
the seven dwarfs, lived happily
together for many years.

Activities

The key below describes the skills
practiced in each activity.

✏️ Spelling and writing

📖 Reading

💬 Speaking

❓ Critical thinking

✳️ Preparation for the Cambridge
Young Learners exams

1 Write the missing letters.

mb bb tsm fo war

1  f o rest

2  d _____ f

3  ri _____ ons

4  co _____

5  hun _____ an

2 **Look and read. Write _T_ (true) or _F_ (false).** 📖 ⬡

A beautiful queen had a baby girl.

The baby's skin was as white as snow, and she had beautiful black hair.

The queen called her baby Snow White.

1 A beautiful queen had a baby girl. ....T............

2 The baby's skin was as white as snow. ....

3 Snow White had beautiful white hair. ....

4 Snow White called the baby Queen. ....

5 The queen called her baby Snow White. ....

3 **Complete the sentences.**
Write a—d.

1 The queen died, and .... d ....

2 The new queen had ....

3 The queen asked the mirror, ...

4 The mirror ....

a a magic mirror.

b said, "You are."

c "Who is the most beautiful woman in the world?"

d the king got married again.

Soon, Snow White was a beautiful young woman.

One day, the queen spoke to her mirror. "Who is the most beautiful woman in the world?" she asked it.

The mirror said, "Snow White is the most beautiful woman in the world."

10

11

1 Soon, Snow White was

a a beautiful young woman.

b a beautiful old woman.

2 One day, the queen spoke to

a Snow White.　　**b** her mirror.

3 The queen asked, "Who is the most

a beautiful woman in the world?"

b beautiful queen in the world?"

4 The mirror said, "Snow White is

a in the forest."

b the most beautiful woman."

5 **Read the questions.**
Write complete answers.

The queen was angry. She didn't want to live with a woman who was more beautiful than her.

"Take Snow White into the forest, and kill her," she said to her huntsman.

1 How did the queen feel when the mirror answered her question?

The queen felt angry.

2 What did the queen want the huntsman to do?

3 What did the huntsman say to Snow White?

6 **Look and read. Put a** ✓ **or a** ✗
in the boxes. 📖 ⬡

1 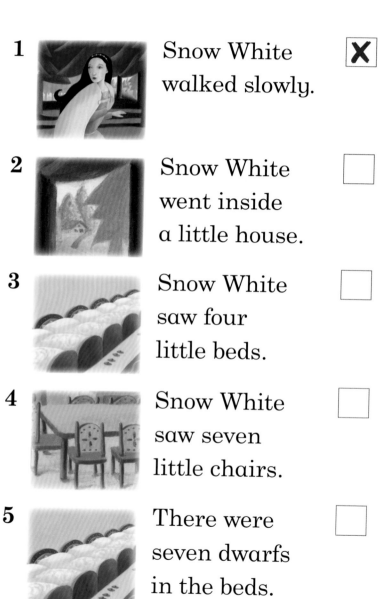 Snow White
walked slowly. ✗

2 Snow White
went inside
a little house. ☐

3 Snow White
saw four
little beds. ☐

4 Snow White
saw seven
little chairs. ☐

5 There were
seven dwarfs
in the beds. ☐

7 Talk about the two pictures with a friend. How are they different? Use the words in the box.

sleeping   tired   not at home
at home   on the beds   near the beds

In picture a, the dwarfs are not at home.

In picture b, the dwarfs are at home.

8 Match the two parts of the sentences. Then, write them on the lines.

1 Snow White went

2 When Snow White woke up,

3 "The bad queen wants

a she saw the seven dwarfs.

b to kill me," said Snow White.

c to sleep on the beds.

1 Snow White went to sleep on the beds.

2 _____

_____

3 _____

_____

9 Write *must* or *mustn't*.

1 "You ⸻ must ⸻ take Snow White into the forest and kill her."

2 "You ⸻ never go home."

3 "I ⸻ speak to people who come to the door."

4 "You ⸻ open the door."

10 **Find the words.**

comb t b o r a p p l e o r f n e u o f o r e s t m b s e m i r r o r s e o i g r i b b o n

comb
mirror
apple
forest
ribbon

11 Write the sentences.

1 (in) (the) (world) (Who) (woman) (is) (the) (most) (beautiful) (?)

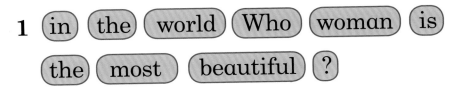

Who is the most beautiful woman in the world?

2 (angry) (was) (queen) (The) (.)

....

3 (Come) (see) (beautiful) (and) (ribbons) (my) (.)

....

....

4 (queen) (a) (ribbon) (round) (The) (Snow White's) (neck) (put) (.)

....

....

12 Circle the correct sentences.

1

a "Snow White is the most beautiful woman in the world," said the mirror.

b "Snow White is living with the dwarfs," said the mirror.

2

a The queen took some combs to Snow White.

b The queen took some combs to the dwarfs.

3

a Snow White put the comb in her hair, and fell to the floor.

b Snow White put the comb in her hair, and it looked very nice.

13 Circle the correct words.

1 The queen **was**/ **were** now very angry.

2 Snow White **went / goed** to the woman, and took an apple.

3 When she ate the apple, she **fell / falled** to the floor.

4 The dwarfs **were / was** very sad, because they could not wake her.

14 **Look at the letters. Write the words.**

1 (s w r d a f)

The _dwarfs_ put Snow White into a glass box.

2 (c e n p r i)

A _____ rode past and saw Snow White in the box.

3 (l s p e n e i g)

He thought she was _____, and he fell in love with her.

4 (d s k i e s)

The prince _____ Snow White. "Please be my wife," he said.

15 Talk to your friend about the bad queen. 💬 ❓

1 What did the queen ask her magic mirror?

She asked, "Who is the most beautiful woman in the world?"

2 Why did the queen take ribbons and a comb to Snow White?

3 What did the prince do when he saw Snow White? Why?

4 What did the queen do when she saw the prince and Snow White?

61

16 **Order the story. Write 1—5.**

_____ The prince kissed Snow White and woke her up.

___1___ The queen had a magic mirror.

_____ The queen tried to kill Snow White.

_____ "Snow White is the most beautiful woman in the world," said the mirror.

_____ The dwarfs were very sad, and they put Snow White in a glass box.

17 Do the crossword.

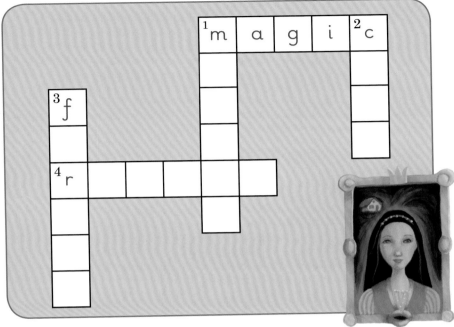

	¹m	a	g	i	²c

³f

⁴r

Across

1 The queen's mirror was . . .

4 The queen put this round Snow White's neck.

Down

1 The queen liked to look in this.

2 The queen left this at the house for Snow White.

3 The dwarfs' house was in this place.

Level 3

Sharks

978–0–241–25382–3 ☐

The Jungle Book

978–0–241–25383–0 ☐

The Red Knight

978–0–241–25384–7 ☐

The Elves and the Shoemaker

978–0–241–25385–4 ☐

Rapunzel

978–0–241–28394–3 ☐

Great Buildings

978–0–241–28400–1 ☐

Minibeasts

978–0–241–28404–9 ☐

Puss in Boots

978–0–241–28407–0 ☐

Jack and the Beanstalk

978–0–241–28397–4 ☐

Hansel and Gretel

978–0–241–29861–9 ☐

The Talent Show

978–0–241–29859–6 ☐

A Great Night!

978–0–241–29863–3 ☐

Bumblebee and the Rock Concert

978-0-241-29867-1 ☐

Where Animals Live

978–0–241–29868–8 ☐

Snow White and the Seven Dwarfs

978–0–241–31955–0 ☐

Ice Worlds

978-0-241-31957-4 ☐

The Pony School News

978-0-241-31611-5 ☐

Now you're ready for Level 4!